For Anna and Charlotte
(and all the WONDERFUL pets you've ever owned!) - T C x

To my mum - J M

LITTLE TIGER PRESS LTD
an imprint of the Little Tiger Group
1 The Coda Centre
189 Munster Road
London SW6 6AW
www.littletiger.co.uk

First published in Great Britain 2017
Text copyright © Tracey Corderoy 2017
Illustrations copyright © Jorge Martín 2017
Tracey Corderoy and Jorge Martín have asserted their rights
to be identified as the author and illustrator of this work
under the Copyright, Designs and Patents Act, 1988
A CIP catalogue record for this book is available
from the British Library

ISBN 978-1-84869-441-5
Printed in China
LTP/1400/1802/0317
10 9 8 7 6 5 4 3 2 1

FAIRY TALE
PETS

TRACEY CORDEROY

JORGE MARTÍN

LITTLE TIGER
LONDON

Bob lived on a nice neat hill,
in a nice neat house, with neat roses.

His dog, called **Rex,** was friendly and smart.
And hardly ever made nasty smells.

And life was perfectly neat and fine,
except . . . they were very, very poor.

"I need to find a job," said Bob.
"But whatever could I do . . . ?"
Then Bob remembered. He loved animals.

And the neighbourhood was FULL of them.

**"That's it! I'll look
after pets!"** he cried. **"Easy!"**

So that very night Bob and Rex stuck posters up all around town. They said:

🦴 NEED HELP WITH YOUR PET? 🦴

THEN BOB (AND REX) ARE FOR YOU!
WE WALK DOGS. WE SIT CATS. WE HOUSE HAMSTERS.
NO PET TOO BIG (OR TOO SMALL).

CALL ROUND TO THE HOUSE ON THE HILL!

"All ready!" said Bob the next day, when . . .

ding dong! the first pet arrived.

"Hi!" beamed a little golden-haired girl. "Could you please look after my baby bear while I'm on holiday?"

"A b-bear!!" gulped Bob. **"Um . . . err . . . "**
He'd been expecting hamsters and bunnies.
"Don't worry," said the girl. "He's such a little poppet!"

And waving goodbye, she skipped away.
But then the 'little poppet' found his voice . . .

"**Goodness!**" cried Bob, staring at the mess.
But the bear didn't care, for *now* he had a SPLINTER!

WAAAA !

No sooner had Bob got the
splinter out when . . .

ding dong!

another pet arrived.

"**I'm Jack!**" said a boy on the doorstep.

"**Can you look after Gabby – my goose?**"

"**Phew,**" smiled Bob. Much easier than a bear!

Jack took some beans from his pocket.

"**Have these in return,**" he said.

"**B-beans??**" puzzled Bob as he took the goose in.

"Now, where shall we **put** her?" he wondered.

But Gabby soon found
the perfect spot for her nest . . .

"Someone's been sitting on my HEAD!" grumbled Baby Bear.
"And she's STILL THERE – LOOK!"

"Don't worry!!" gasped Bob. "We'll soon get her off!"
But the goose would not be moved.

She fluttered and flapped.

She **pecked** and **squawked.**

CRASH!

"Good heavens!!" spluttered Bob.

"Too noisy!" cried Baby Bear.

WAAAA!

Poor Rex had barely tidied up, when . . .

ding
dooooong!

"**Not MORE pets!**" groaned Bob.
  With a heavy sigh, he opened the door
to see a rather hairy lady glaring back.

"**Here,**" she said in a growly voice.
"**Take these nice, quiet billy goats.**"

"**N-no, wait!**" pleaded Bob.
"**We haven't room for all three!**"

But the goats were already inside . . .

TRIP TRAP!

TRIP
TRAP!

...went their great

clumpy hooves,

trampling over teapots,

trooping over tables and—

"OWWWWW!

They trod on my TOES!"
squealed Baby Bear.
"Waaaaaaaaaa!!!"

What a RUMPUS!

"Shhhhhhhhhh,"
whispered Bob,
"or you'll scare the goose!"

But it was **too late** . . .

"HONK!" Gabby hooted.
And out tumbled LOTS more eggs.

They **thumped** and **bumped** and **bashed** and **crashed.**

But when things could not get ANY worse,
three little pigs zoomed up.

"Our – um – puppy needs a walk," the leader cried.
"He's ever so friendly. Honest!"

Bob looked at the puppy. It was positively **HUGE**.
"I'm sorry – we're f-full!" he stuttered.

But the puppy just opened
its big wolfy mouth,

full of big, sharp wolfy teeth.

Then it **huffed** and it **puffed** . . .

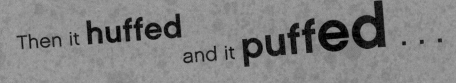

. . . and it **BLEW THE HOUSE** *DOWN!!!*

Meeeh!

WAAAAAAA!

HONK HONK HONK!

"**Oh Rex!**" gasped Bob.
"**I'm done with pet-sitting.**"

The problem was, what **else** could he do . . . ?

Then out of his pocket fell one
of Jack's beans

"That's it! I'll be a gardener!"
Bob decided, planting all the beans at once.

Soon they would grow.
Then he'd sell them at market.
And he and Rex would live happily ever after!

"HOORAY!" cheered Bob
with a great big smile.

What could possibly
go wrong?!